Grasslands and Prairies

Wetlands

This book is dedicated to all future environmentalists, ecologists, activists, artists, naturalists and custodians of Earth and its precious biodiversity. Also to my boys, Leo and Gil, for your support and suggestions.

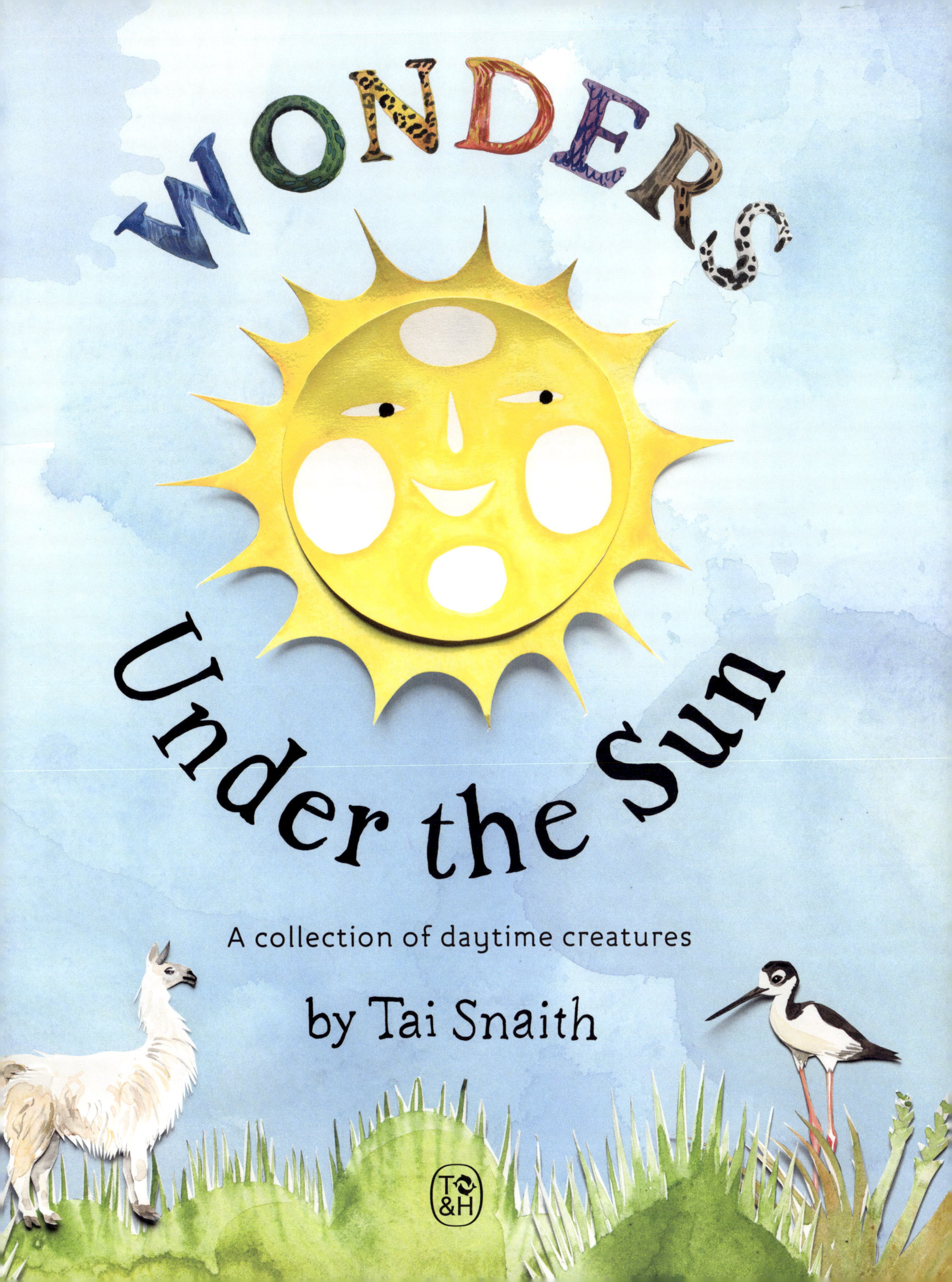
WONDERS
Under the Sun
A collection of daytime creatures
by Tai Snaith
T&H

Who you'll

4 Introduction

6 **Precious Pollinators**

8 **Happy Hoppers**

10 **Tiny Tweeters**

12 **Sun Seekers**

14 **Gangly Gang**

16 **Homebodies**

18 **Legless Legends**

20 **Magic Mimics**

find inside

22 Spikey Spunks

24 Swingers and Clingers

26 Spotted Bottoms

28 Horny Herbivores

30 Woolly Wanderers

32 Growlers and Howlers

34 Big, Bold and Beautiful

36 Ways we can help

38 Creature details

Introduction

In this book, you will find page after page of wondrous wildlife. These creatures live on this Earth with us, under the same Sun. Like us, they are mostly diurnal (active during daylight hours), or crepuscular (active during dusk and dawn). You will find them in different habitats all over the world: from grassy plains to humid mossy rainforests, soggy wetlands to flowery meadows, rocky mountain tops to scorching hot deserts and savannas. From the tiniest pollinators to the heaviest giants, they all play important roles in Earth's biodiversity – the rich mixture of living things that help each other, and us, to survive.

Some of them are so weird and wonderful that you may not believe they are real! Like the giant dead-leaf mantis, which can fold its legs to look like an angry face and seem much bigger and scarier than it really is. Or the green anaconda, which can swallow a pig or a sheep whole – sometimes even a jaguar! And some, like the Cuvier tropid snail or the black-crowned crane, are so marvellous to look at that you might think an artist designed them. It can often be hard to figure out the size of these animals in books so on each page there is something to compare them to for scale, like an ear or a hand, a little girl or a tall basketball player. On page after page we see that nature is full of incredible surprises and wondrous beauty.

As an artist, I can't help but see the beauty of nature everywhere I look. This book is like a visual diary of all my favourite creatures. But many of these amazing creatures are in serious trouble. Next to some of the animals' names in the book, you might notice an icon. This means these animals are vulnerable, endangered, or critically endangered.

One of the main reasons animals are vulnerable or endangered is because they are losing their homes, or habitats. At the start and end of the book, I have illustrated a few of the habitats in which these wondrous creatures live. Places like old-growth forests and rainforests are especially important as they have such rich biodiversity, with many species of plants and animals living together. As humans, we must help protect these habitats, regenerate those that are damaged or create new ones where we can.

Ask yourself, 'What if we let these creatures die out?' Then ask, 'What if we do *everything* we can right now to help them to survive?' There is a list at the end of this book with some ideas for things you can do in your own home or community to help protect your local wildlife and provide more places for plants and animals to live. You might also like to keep an eye out for some of these wonders under the Sun that live near you and begin your own visual diary. Paying attention is the start of taking action.

Key

- V Vulnerable
- E Endangered
- C Critically endangered

Precious Pollinators

We help plants transfer pollen

1. Spotted cucumber beetle

2. Swollen-thighed beetle

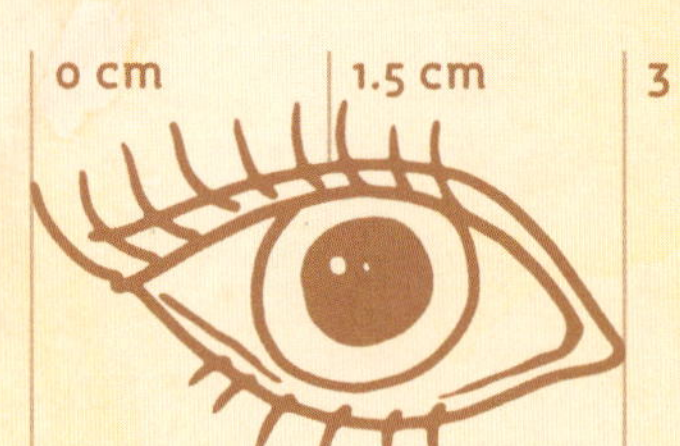

6. Common house fly

7. Confusing bumblebee

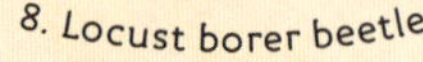

8. Locust borer beetle

11. Comma butterfly

12. Eighty-eight or -nine butterfly

13. Black horsefly

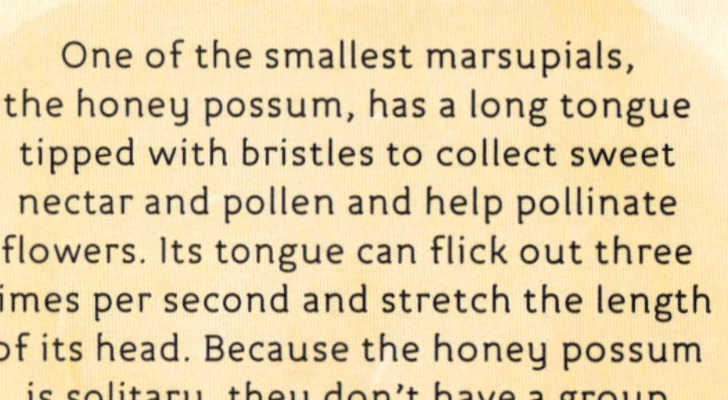

One of the smallest marsupials, the honey possum, has a long tongue tipped with bristles to collect sweet nectar and pollen and help pollinate flowers. Its tongue can flick out three times per second and stretch the length of its head. Because the honey possum is solitary, they don't have a group name. If they did, what would you call a group of possums? Maybe a party?

16. Giant honey bee

14. Chinese peacock butterfly

15. Honey possum

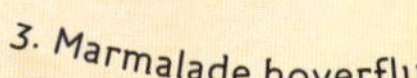
3. Marmalade hoverfly

4. Common blue-banded bee

5. Dusky-winged hoverfly

9. Arctic bumblebee

The Arctic bumblebee has such thick hair it can stay warm in freezing temperatures. It also has large 'flight' muscles, which it 'shivers' or shakes quickly to generate extra warmth. A group of bees is called a swarm.

10. Himalayan giant honey bee

17. Monarch butterfly

19. Hummingbird hawkmouth

18. Tiny sunbird

Happy Hoppers

We jump from place to place

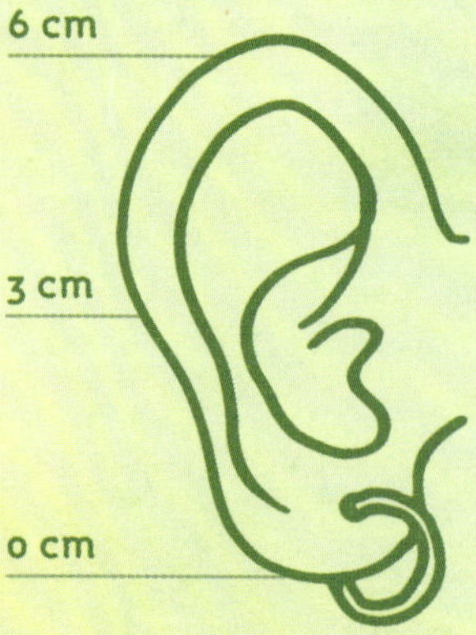

20. Karrie's peacock spider

The jumping spider can leap 10 to 50 times its body length. That's like a kid being able to jump over a multi-storey building! These spiders have 8 eyes and can see in all directions. A group of spiders is called a clutter or cluster.

6 cm
3 cm
0 cm

21. Reticulated poison-dart frog

22. Black-spotted peacock spider

23. Rainbow grasshopper

24. Key's matchstick grasshopper E

25. Giant jumping spider

26. Greenhouse camel cricket

27. Sword-bearing conehead

28. Longan lanternfly

29. Gumleaf katydid

30. Short-horned grasshopper

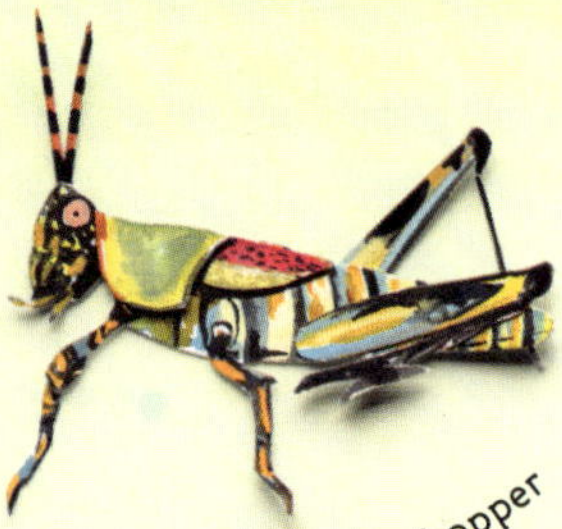

31. Elegant grasshopper

32. Horse lubber grasshopper

33. Tien Shan birch mouse

34. Four-toed jerboa

35. Woodland jumping mouse

130 cm
65 cm
0 cm
36. Eurasian hoopoe
37. Mountain cottontail rabbit
38. Pygmy rabbit
39. Verreaux's sifaka
C
40. Dassie
41. Klipspringer
42. Red-legged pademelon
43. Bennett's wallaby
44. Red kangaroo
45. Eastern grey kangaroo

Tiny Tweeters

We chirp, trill and whistle

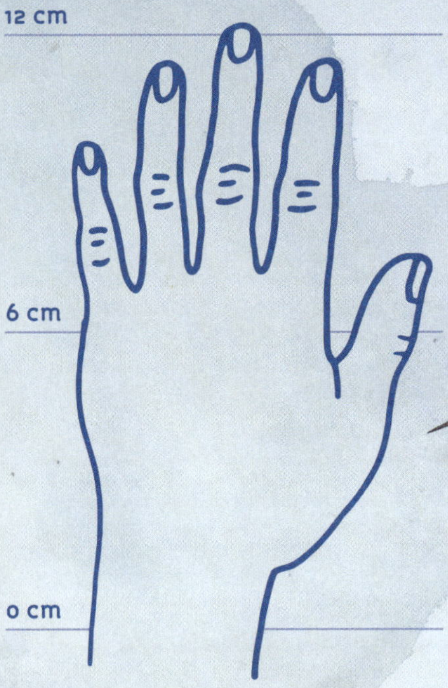

12 cm
6 cm
0 cm

46. Bee hummingbird

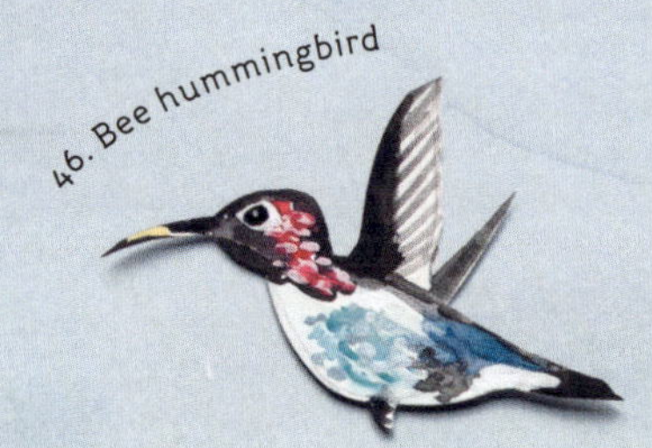

The bee hummingbird is the tiniest bird in the world. Its egg is the size of a coffee bean and weighs no more than half a paperclip! It sips nectar from up to 1500 flowers a day. Its wings sound like a buzzing bee and it has a high, piping song. A group of hummingbirds is called a bouquet or charm.

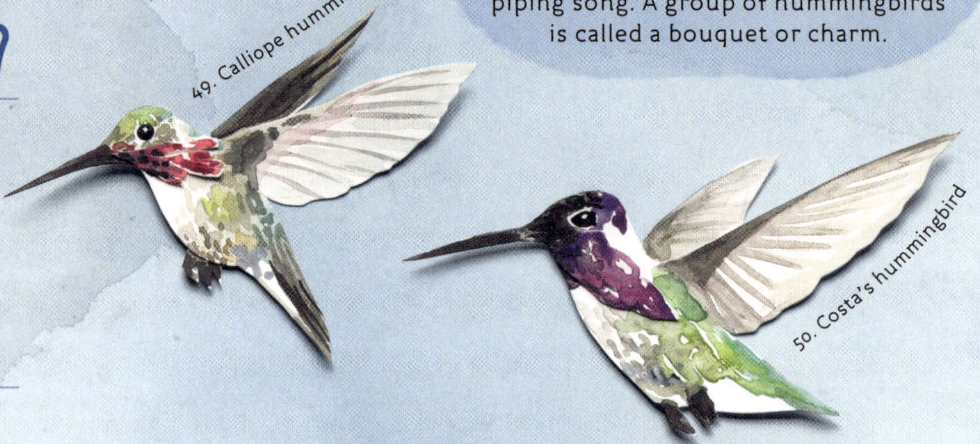

49. Calliope hummingbird
50. Costa's hummingbird

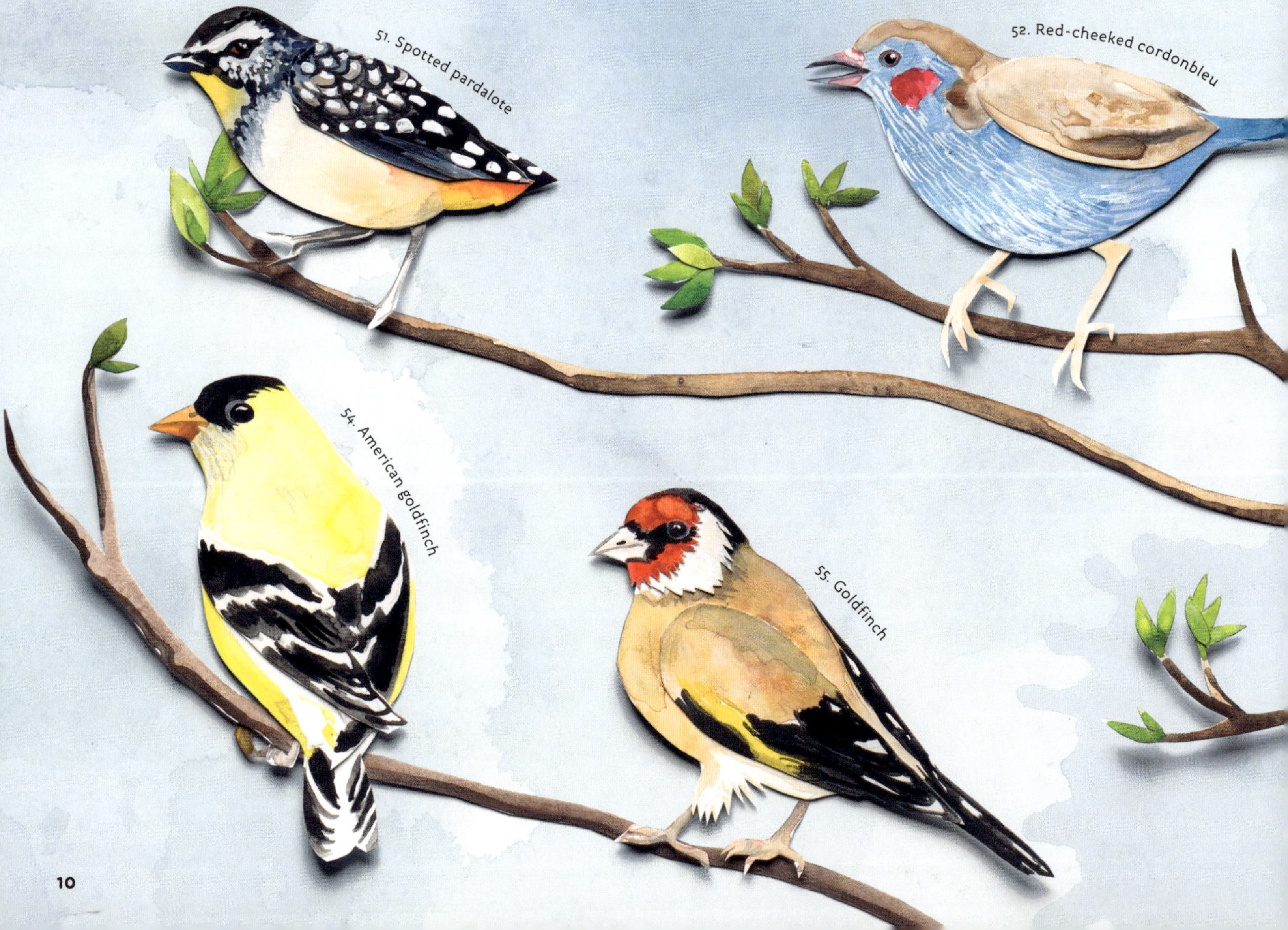

51. Spotted pardalote
52. Red-cheeked cordonbleu
54. American goldfinch
55. Goldfinch

47. Goldcrest
48. Bananaquit
53. Diamond firetail
58. Superb fairywren
56. Verdin
57. Pink robin

Sun Seekers

We get our energy from the sun

59. Northern sandy dung beetle

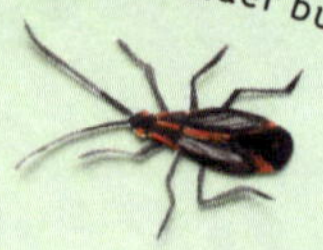

61. Boxelder bug

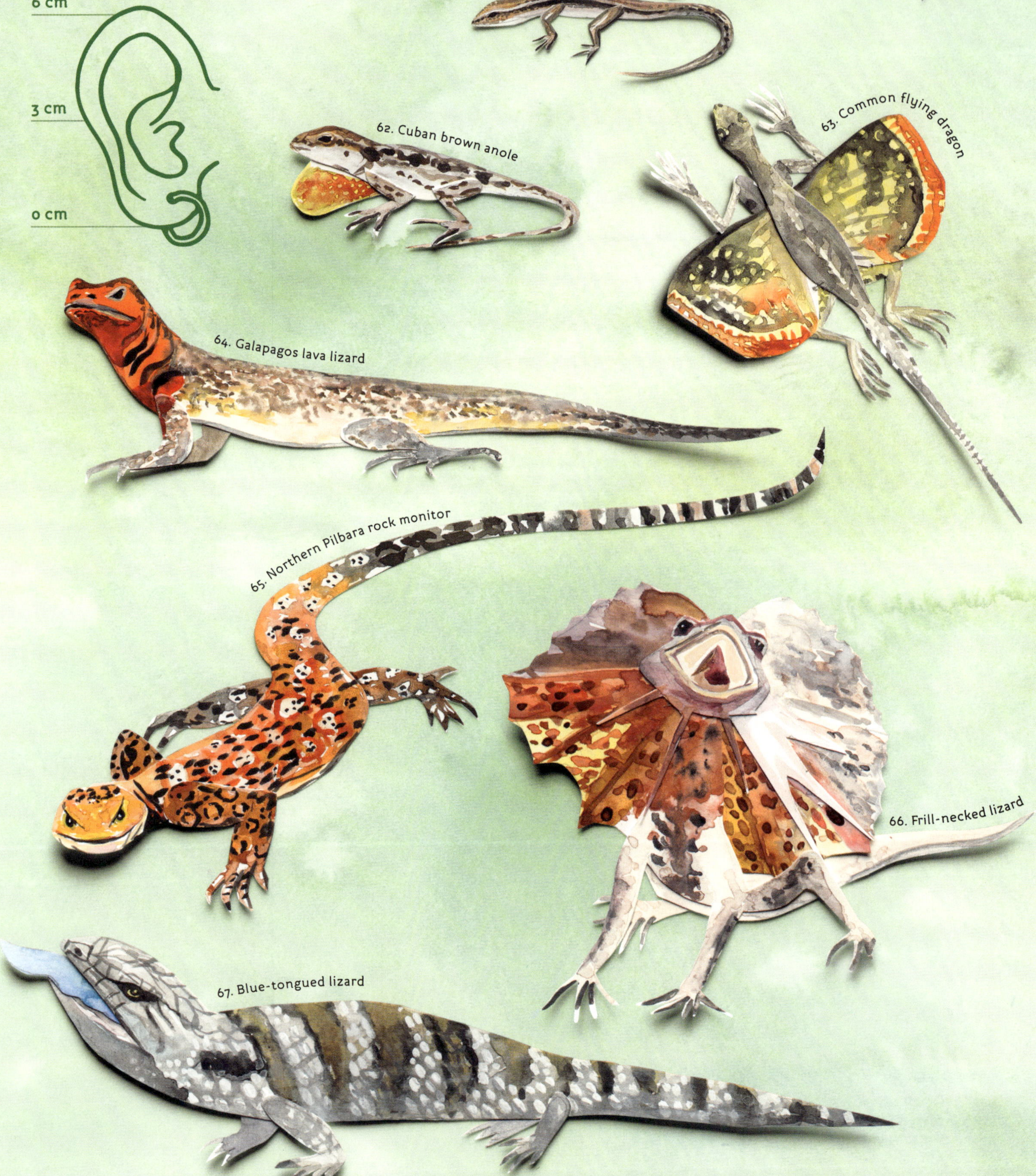

6 cm
3 cm
0 cm
60. Delicate garden skink
62. Cuban brown anole
63. Common flying dragon
64. Galapagos lava lizard
65. Northern Pilbara rock monitor
66. Frill-necked lizard
67. Blue-tongued lizard

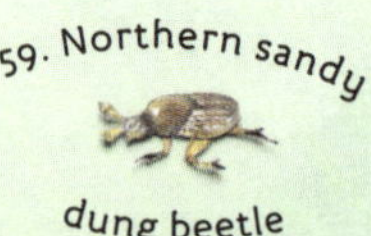

Saltwater crocodiles were basking in the sun when dinosaurs roamed the Earth – they've changed little since then. They can also live for up to 80 years. That makes them one deadly living dinosaur! A group of crocodiles on land is called a bask and a group in the water is called a float.

Gangly Gang

We lay eggs and have long legs

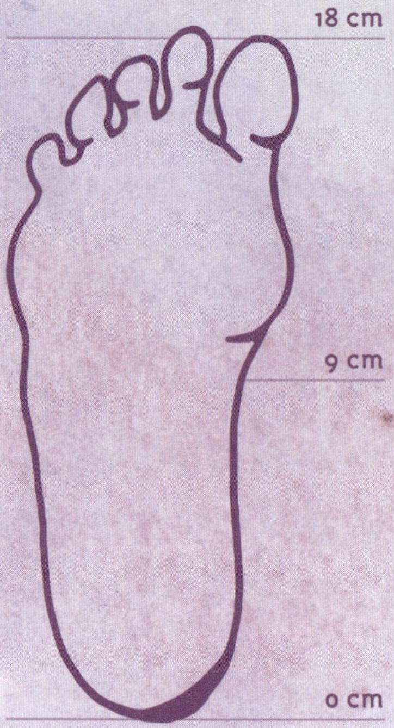

18 cm

9 cm

0 cm

78. Tiger cranefly

77. Daddy-long-legs spider

80. Arizona unicorn mantis

79. Yellow flying stick

81. Zebra-tailed lizard

82. Wandering violin mantis

83. Giant long-legged katydid

84. Jungle nymph

The jungle nymph is the heaviest stick insect in the world and lays the biggest eggs of all insects.

After a female cassowary lays her eggs, the male sits on them for 50 days, during which time he doesn't eat or drink. When the eggs hatch, he raises the chicks for the next 9 months. The cassowary is also one of the only birds to have killed a human, using their muscular, powerful legs with clawed feet. A group of cassowaries is called a dash.

Homebodies

We carry our homes on our backs

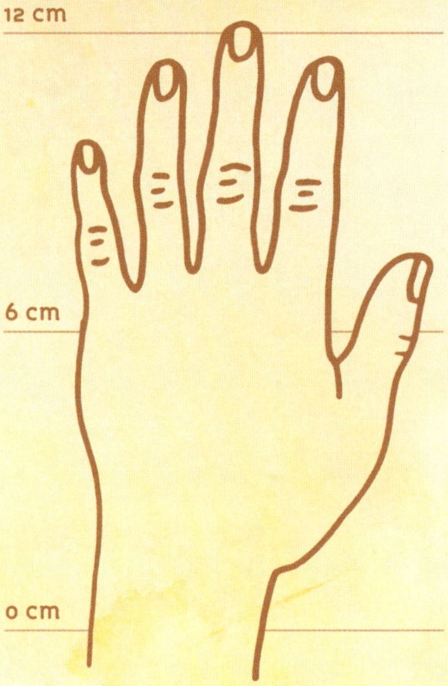

12 cm

6 cm

0 cm

96. World's smallest land snail

97. Hairy snail

98. Garden snail

99. Brown-lipped snail

100. Cuban painted snail C

101. Ecuadorian hermit crab

102. Ruggie

103. Candy-cane snail

104. Australian land hermit crab

105. Cuvier tropid snail

106. Strawberry hermit crab

107. Giant flat snail

108. Speckled dwarf tortoise E

109. Black-knobbed map turtle

110. Ornate box turtle

111. Yellow-bellied slider

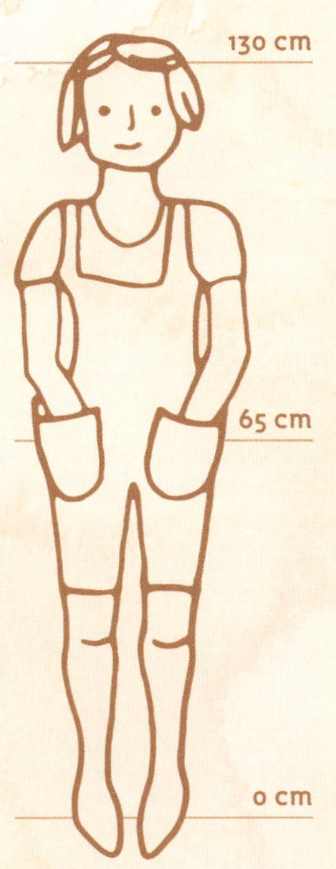

112. Giant African snail

113. Diamondback terrapin V

114. Painted wood turtle

115. Californian desert tortoise V

116. Star tortoise V

117. North American wood turtle E

118. Leopard tortoise

119. Alligator snapping turtle V

The Galapagos tortoise is the largest tortoise on Earth. They mate during the hot season and the female lays up to 16 eggs the size of tennis balls. Tortoises rest for 16 hours a day and can survive up to a year without food or water. A group of tortoises is called a creep.

121. Galapagos tortoise E / C

120. Aldabra giant tortoise V

Legless Legends

We have no arms or legs

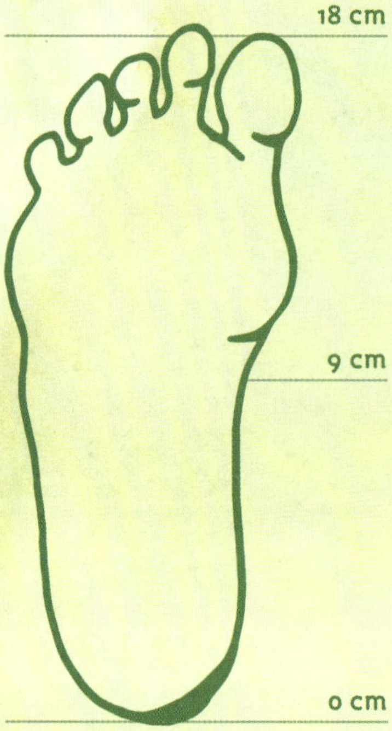

18 cm

9 cm

0 cm

122. California legless lizard

123. Striped legless lizard

124. Darevsky's viper C

125. Slender glass lizard

126. Red corn snake

127. Burton's legless lizard

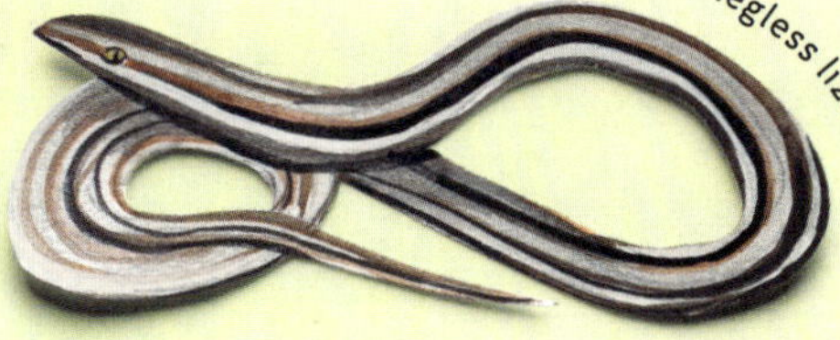

128. African bush viper

129. Common death adder

130. Antiguan racer C

131. California kingsnake

132. Wagner's viper C

The green anaconda is the heaviest snake in the world and females can grow up to 9 metres long. They aren't venomous – they catch prey in their strong jaws then squeeze them to death. They unhinge their jaws to swallow whole prey such as deer, capybaras and even jaguars. A group of anacondas is called a bed or knot.

Magic Mimics

We blend and pretend

The giant dead-leaf mantis mimics a dry leaf for camouflage, but if it's threatened, it can arrange its body to look like a big scary face. This is called a 'deimatic display', designed to scare off predators. A group of mantises is called a congregation.

154. Lined leaf-tailed gecko

158. Panther chameleon

155. Henkel's leaf-tailed gecko V

156. Tokay gecko

157. California ground squirrel

159. Veiled chameleon

Both the arctic fox and the arctic hare are pure white. This makes them almost invisible to predators in their snowy habitat.

160. Arctic fox

161. Arctic hare

162. Polar bear V

163. Okapi E

Spikey Spunks

We have spikes and crazy hairstyles

Echidnas are usually seen hunting for ants or termites but they also like to swim, lifting their long snouts up to breathe. When a female is ready to mate, a queue of male echidnas follows her in an 'echidna train'. If an echidna is threatened it digs into the ground so only its sharp spikes are exposed. A group of echidnas is called a parade.

167. Armadillo lizard
168. Lowland streaked tenrec
169. Thorny devil
173. Golden spiny mouse
174. Spiny turtle E
172. Sulphur-crested cockatoo
178. Black-crowned crane V
177. Bare-faced curassow V

Swingers and Clingers

We hang around in trees

Borneo orangutans need trees for food and shelter. They often eat with their feet so they can swing with their arms. Orangutans are the largest animals to live in trees. A group of orangutans is called a buffoonery.

Spotted Bottoms

We have lots of beauty marks

196. Western spotted skunk

201. Tiger quoll

203. Spotted linsang

202. Eastern quoll E

Quolls are hunters, preying on rabbits, rodents and other small animals or insects, and even climbing trees to hunt sleeping birds. Their spots help them camouflage in the shadows to confuse their prey. The bite of the spotted-tail quoll is the second strongest in the world, beaten only by the Tasmanian devil. Quolls don't have an official group name; can you think of a good one? Maybe a flash?

197. Spotted lanternfly
198. Red avadavat
199. Eastern spotted salamander
200. Spotted wood kingfisher
206. Common genet
205. Temminck's tragopan
204. African civet
210. Helmeted guinea fowl
209. Spotted hyena
208. Brazilian tapir baby V
211. Visayan spotted deer E
217. American appaloosa horse
216. Sika deer

Horny Herbivores

We have horns and eat plants

When bongos hurry through thick vegetation, they lift their heads so their horns lie flat along their backs. Sometimes bongos nibble at charred trees struck by lightning, perhaps to get salt or minerals. A group of bongos is called a herd.

Woolly Wanderers

Our hair is made into wool

Bactrian camels can wander nearly 50 kilometres a day. They can survive for months without a drink, then swallow up to 130 litres of water at a time. Their thick, woolly coats keep them warm in winter, then they shed them for summer. A group of camels is called a caravan or train.

Growlers and Howlers

We grumble and prowl

The tough honey badger is not an animal you want to pick a fight with! They have been known to kill and eat deadly snakes, like king cobras, and can withstand hundreds of bee stings to get to the larvae within a hive. A group of badgers is called a cete or clan.

The wolverine has such a good sense of smell it can detect food (animals or plants) 6 metres under the snow. Their jaws are strong enough to eat big bones. A member of the weasel family, wolverines don't howl but instead growl, snarl or chuckle. A group of wolverines is called a gang.

Big, Bold and Beautiful

We are giants of our kind

18 cm

9 cm

0 cm

261. Goliath beetle

262. Giant grasshopper

263. Sea slater

267. Goliath birdeater spider

270. Giant African millipede

271. African giant swallowtail

274. Goliath birdwing

275. Queen Alexandra birdwing butterfly E

The largest land animal on Earth is the African elephant. The heaviest elephant on record weighed nearly 11 tonnes and was close to 4 metres tall at the shoulder. That's almost the weight and height of a double-decker bus! A group of elephants is called a herd or memory.

Ways we can help

Many of the species listed as vulnerable or endangered are disappearing due to habitat loss. As cities expand and land is cleared for crops and human development, habitats and the animals that live there are destroyed. Once a species goes extinct, it is gone forever.

How can you provide a little more wild space for nature to creep back in? Your actions, however small, can help create or save animals' habitats. Here are some ways to start today.

1. Many plant species, including vegetables and fruit or nut trees, rely on bees to pollinate their flowers. Land clearing and bushfires are destroying bee habitats, and insecticides are killing both native bees and honeybees. Why not make your garden a haven for bees? Put a bowl of water out for thirsty bees in summer. Grow flowering native plants to provide bees with nectar and pollen.

2. Leave the leaves! Fallen leaves and mulch feed many tiny organisms and provide shelter for insects, other invertebrates and even small reptiles. These are a vital part of an ecosystem and add to biodiversity. Try introducing some shelter for small creatures, such as lizards by putting rocks and hollow logs in dry, sunny areas.

3. Put some nesting boxes high in the trees for birds and possums. When old trees are cut down or fall down, birds and possums lose their nesting hollows. By adding a nesting box up in a tree, you are replacing a tree hollow and providing an animal or bird with a safe home for their babies.

4. Paint a sign and make your voice heard. Are you passionate about slowing climate change or protecting native forests? Join a protest like School Strike 4 Climate, get noisy and become part of the revolution to save the planet.

5. Most towns and suburbs have groups that look after local bushland or nature reserves. These groups remove weeds and rubbish and plant native species, allowing the bush to regenerate. Soon, native birds and animals start to return. You could join one of these groups, or even raise money at school to donate to one. Ask your local parks authority or council for information.

6. If you have a pet cat, keep it inside altogether, or at least at night. Most of the smaller marsupials and birds on the threatened or endangered list are there because of pet and feral cats or foxes. Your kitty might be cuddly and cute in your bedroom, but outside it's a killer!

7. Try to reuse and recycle paper, and always buy recycled paper products. Many of our old-growth forests are still being cut down, destroying important habitats. The Forest Stewardship Council (FSC) website (fsc.org) lists sustainable paper brands. Ask your principal if your school is using recycled or FSC-approved paper. If not, you could help research a better option.

8. Many Indigenous groups recognise more than the four European seasons you might know. These seasons are marked by when certain plants bloom, or tadpoles hatch, or birds appear or disappear or start nesting. Learn about the Indigenous seasons in your area by contacting your local Aboriginal land council. Another useful resource is the Bureau of Meteorology's Indigenous Weather Knowledge website (bom.gov.au/iwk/). You can spot seasonal signs in your neighbourhood by observing plants and animals closely, recording what you see and researching further – then share what you know in a story or a chart.

Creature details

Precious Pollinators

1. **Spotted cucumber beetle** | *Diabrotica undecimpunctata* | Insect | Found in agricultural areas in North America
2. **Swollen-thighed beetle** | *Oedemera nobilis* | Insect | Found on flowers in western and southern Europe
3. **Marmalade hoverfly** | *Episyrphus balteatus* | Insect | Found on flowers in North America and Eurasia
4. **Common blue-banded bee** | *Amegilla cingulata* | Insect | Found on flowers in Australia, Papua New Guinea, Indonesia, East Timor, Malaysia and India

5. **Dusky-winged hoverfly** | *Ocyptamus fuscipennis* | Insect | Found in forest from North America to Cuba
6. **Common house fly** | *Musca domestica* | Insect | Found in urban and rural areas worldwide, laying their eggs in human garbage and faeces
7. **Confusing bumblebee** | *Bombus perplexus* | Insect | Found in woods, wetlands, parks and gardens in North America
8. **Locust borer beetle** | *Megacyllene robiniae* | Insect | Found anywhere black locust trees grow in North America
9. **Arctic bumblebee** | *Bombus polaris* | Insect | Found in tundra in northern Alaska, USA; Canada; Scandinavia and Russia
10. **Himalayan giant honey bee** | *Apis laboriosa* | Insect | Found in mountainous places and high-altitude cliffs in Nepal, Bhutan, India and Yunnan province, China
11. **Comma butterfly** | *Polygonia c-album* | Insect | Found where stinging nettles and other food plants grow in woodland and gardens in Europe
12. **Eighty-eight or -nine butterfly** | *Diaethria neglecta* | Insect | Found in rainforest and cloud-forest with Tema trees, on which they lay eggs, from Panama to Bolivia
13. **Black horsefly** | *Tabanus atratus* | Insect | Found in eastern North America, where they lay their eggs in moist places and feed on mammals
14. **Chinese peacock butterfly** | *Papilio bianor* | Insect | Found where food plants for larvae grow in forests and parks from south-eastern Russia to Japan and South-East Asia
15. **Honey possum** | *Tarsipes rostratus* | Marsupial mammal | Found in banksia woodland in south-western Western Australia
16. **Giant honey bee** | *Apis dorsata* | Insect | Found on flowers in southern Asia, from India to Indonesia, nesting in forest, cliffs and sometimes cities
17. **Monarch butterfly** | *Danaus plexippus* | Insect | Found on milkweed in open country from North and South America to Indonesia and Western Europe
18. **Tiny sunbird** | *Cinnyris minullus* | Bird | Found in subtropical and tropical forest and moist lowlands in western-central and central Africa
19. **Hummingbird hawkmoth** | *Macroglossum stellatarum* | Insect | Found in woodland and gardens in southern Europe and Asia, northern Africa (winter) and northern Europe and Russia (summer)

Happy Hoppers

20. **Karrie's peacock spider** | *Maratus karrie* | Arachnid | Found in forest in western and eastern Australia
21. **Reticulated poison-dart frog** | *Ranitomeya ventrimaculata* | Amphibian | Found in rainforest trees in north-western South America
22. **Black-spotted peacock spider** | *Maratus nigromaculatus* | Arachnid | Found on green shrubs in Queensland, Australia
23. **Rainbow grasshopper** | *Dactylotum bicolor* | Insect | Found in prairies, desert grassland and alfalfa fields in North and Central America

24. **Key's matchstick grasshopper** | *Keyacris scurra* | Insect | Found in native grassland in southern Australia | E
25. **Giant jumping spider** | *Hyllus giganteus* | Arachnid | Found in vegetation, under rocks and bark from Australia to Sumatra
26. **Greenhouse camel cricket** | *Tachycines asynamorus* | Insect | Found in Asia but prefers heated greenhouses
27. **Sword-bearing conehead** | *Neoconocephalus ensiger* | Insect | Found in weeds or high grass in North America
28. **Longan lanternfly** | *Pyrops candelaria* | Insect | Found on trees such as longan and lychee in South-East Asia
29. **Gumleaf katydid** | *Torbia viridissima* | Insect | Found in eastern Australia in eucalyptus trees, on which they feed
30. **Short-horned grasshopper** | *Monachidium lunum* | Insect | Found in Brazil, Suriname and French Guiana
31. **Elegant grasshopper** | *Zonocerus elegans* | Insect | Found in grassland, gardens and cultivated fields in southern Africa
32. **Horse lubber grasshopper** | *Taeniopoda eques* | Insect | Found in North and Central America in desert brush and grassland
33. **Tien Shan birch mouse** | *Sicista tianshanica* | Mammal | Found on or near mountains in forests and meadows in China, Kazakhstan and Kyrgyzstan
34. **Four-toed jerboa** | *Allactaga tetradactyla* | Mammal | Found in clay desert, semidesert and coastal salt marshes of north-eastern Africa, the Arabian Peninsula, and south-western and central Asia
35. **Woodland jumping mouse** | *Napaeozapus insignis* | Mammal | Found in forest and woodland in north-eastern North America
36. **Eurasian hoopoe** | *Upupa epops* | Bird | Found foraging in grassland and nesting in woods and hedgerows in Europe, Asia, North Africa and northern sub-Saharan Africa
37. **Mountain cottontail rabbit** | *Sylvilagus nuttallii* | Mammal | Found in brushy or wooded land with sagebrush in western USA
38. **Pygmy rabbit** | *Brachylagus idahoensis* | Mammal | Found in sagebrush country in western USA
39. **Verreaux's sifaka** | *Propithecus verreauxi* | Mammal | Found in deciduous and evergreen forest throughout western and south-western Madagascar | C
40. **Dassie** | *Procavia capensis* | Mammal | Found in desert, savanna and scrub forest in Africa and the Arabian Peninsula
41. **Klipspringer** | *Oreotragus oreotragus* | Mammal | Found in rocky habitat in eastern, south-western and southern Africa
42. **Red-legged pademelon** | *Thylogale stigmatica* | Marsupial mammal | Found in rainforest, wet sclerophyll forest and dry vine scrub forest in eastern Australia and Papua New Guinea

43. **Bennett's wallaby** | *Macropus rufogriseus* | Marsupial mammal | Found in eucalypt forest and open woodland in Tasmania and eastern mainland Australia
44. **Red kangaroo** | *Osphranter rufus* | Marsupial mammal | Found on open plains throughout Australia, except along the eastern coast
45. **Eastern grey kangaroo** | *Macropus giganteus* | Marsupial mammal | Found in open woodland and grassland in eastern Australia

Tiny Tweeters

46. **Bee hummingbird** | *Mellisuga helenae* | Bird | Found in wetlands, moist and dry forest, pine forest and cactus scrub in Cuba and the Bahamas
47. **Goldcrest** | *Regulus regulus* | Bird | Found in conifer and mixed woodland from Britain and across Europe to Japan
48. **Bananaquit** | *Coereba flaveola* | Bird | Found in forest edges, woodland and gardens in tropical and subtropical Central and South America
49. **Calliope hummingbird** | *Selasphorus calliope* | Bird | Found in pine–oak forest, mountain meadows and thickets from eastern North America to Mexico
50. **Costa's hummingbird** | *Calypte costae* | Bird | Found in desert scrub, chaparral and sage scrub from south-eastern North America to Mexico
51. **Spotted pardalote** | *Pardalotus punctatus* | Bird | Found in eucalypt forest and woodland, nesting in creek banks in Australia
52. **Red-cheeked cordonbleu** | *Uraeginthus bengalus* | Bird | Found in open habitats in central Africa

53. **Diamond firetail** | *Stagonopleura guttata* | Bird | Found in open grassy woodland, mallee and grassland in south-eastern Australia
54. **American goldfinch** | *Spinus tristis* | Bird | Found in weedy fields, orchards, gardens and farmland from Canada to Mexico
55. **Goldfinch** | *Carduelis carduelis* | Bird | Found in weedy grassland, farmland and gardens in Europe, northern Africa, central Asia, and now in Australia and New Zealand
56. **Verdin** | *Auriparus flaviceps* | Bird | Found in thorny desert scrub with some trees in southern North America
57. **Pink robin** | *Petroica rodinogaster* | Bird | Found in dense wet rainforest and tall open eucalypt forest in Victoria and Tasmania, Australia
58. **Superb fairywren** | *Malurus cyaneus* | Bird | Found in parks, gardens and open woodland and heaths in south-eastern Australia

Sun Seekers

59. **Northern sandy dung beetle** | *Euoniticellus intermedius* | Insect | Found in open areas and pasture with dung, originally in eastern Africa, now introduced to Australia
60. **Delicate garden skink** | *Lampropholis delicata* | Reptile | Found in rainforest, coastal vegetation, bushland and suburban gardens, originally in Australia, now introduced to New Zealand and Hawaii, USA
61. **Boxelder bug** | *Boisea trivittata* | Insect | Found around boxelder trees in western North America
62. **Cuban brown anole** | *Norops sagrei* | Reptile | Found in open vegetation and moist forests from southern USA to Mexico and the Caribbean
63. **Common flying dragon** | *Draco volans* | Reptile | Found in tropical rainforests in southern India and South-East Asia, the Philippines and Borneo
64. **Galapagos lava lizard** | *Microlophus albemarlensis* | Reptile | Found in dry lowland areas of the Galapagos Islands
65. **Northern Pilbara rock monitor** | *Varanus pilbarensis* | Reptile | Found in rocky habitats in the northern Pilbara in Western Australia
66. **Frill-necked lizard** | *Chlamydosaurus kingii* | Reptile | Found in trees in dry sclerophyll forest and semi-arid to tropical woodlands in northern Australia and southern New Guinea
67. **Blue-tongued lizard** | *Tiliqua scincoides* | Reptile | Found in semidesert, woodland, scrubland and suburban areas in Australia
68. **Oriental garden lizard** | *Calotes versicolor* | Reptile | Found in undergrowth in open habitats, shrublands and urban areas in the Middle East, southern Asia and South-East Asia
69. **European green lizard** | *Lacerta viridis* | Reptile | Found in dense vegetation in many habitats in south-eastern Europe
70. **Shingleback lizard** | *Tiliqua rugosa* | Reptile | Found in semi-arid plains and woodland in Australia, and coastal areas of Western and South Australia
71. **Lace monitor** | *Varanus varius* | Reptile | Found in dry forest and woodland in eastern Australia

72. **Australian water dragon** | *Intellagama lesueurii* | Reptile | Found near water throughout eastern Australia
73. **Iguana** | *Iguana iguana* | Reptile | Found near water in rainforest and forest trees in Central and South America
74. **Sailfin water lizard** | *Hydrosaurus pustulatus* | Reptile | Found in lowland tropical forest and cultivated areas in the Philippines | V
75. **American alligator** | *Alligator mississippiensis* | Reptile | Found in fresh water in North America
76. **Saltwater crocodile** | *Crocodylus porosus* | Reptile | Found in coastal waters or rivers, billabongs and swamps from Sri Lanka to Australia

Gangly gang

77. **Daddy-long-legs spider** | *Pholcus phalangioides* | Arachnid | Found in houses and caves worldwide
78. **Tiger cranefly** | *Nephrotoma flavescens* | Insect | Found in moist environments in most of the northern hemisphere, except for North America
79. **Yellow flying stick** | *Necroscia annulipes* | Insect | Found in rainforest in Malaysia and Indonesia
80. **Arizona unicorn mantis** | *Pseudovates arizonae* | Insect | Found in bushes and trees in southern USA and Mexico
81. **Zebra-tailed lizard** | *Callisaurus draconoides* | Reptile | Found in desert or semi-arid rocky habitats with sandy soil in south-western USA and northern Mexico
82. **Wandering violin mantis** | *Gongylus gongylodes* | Insect | Found in open sunny clearings and grassland in India and Sri Lanka
83. **Giant long-legged katydid** | *Macrolyristes corporalis* | Insect | Found in tropical rainforest in Malaysia
84. **Jungle nymph** | *Heteropteryx dilatata* | Insect | Found in tropical rainforest in Malaysia
85. **Black-necked stilt** | *Himantopus mexicanus* | Bird | Found in marshes, mudflats, and beside lakes and rivers in the South Pacific, Africa, Eurasia, the Americas and Australia
86. **Long-billed curlew** | *Numenius americanus* | Bird | Found in grassland in western USA, as far north as southern Canada, and Mexico
87. **Black-necked stork** | *Ephippiorhynchus asiaticus* | Bird | Found in tropical ponds and wetlands from northern Australia through South-East Asia to India and Pakistan
88. **American flamingo** | *Phoenicopterus ruber* | Bird | Found in mudflats and coastal lagoons in Central and South America and the Caribbean
89. **Grey heron** | *Ardea cinerea* | Bird | Found beside inlets and estuaries, freshwater rivers, streams, lakes and marshes in Eurasia and Africa
90. **Secretary bird** | *Sagittarius serpentarius* | Bird | Found in semi-arid savanna, grassland, scrub and lightly wooded areas of sub-Saharan Africa | E
91. **Kori bustard** | *Ardeotis kori* | Bird | Found in savanna, grassland and semidesert in eastern and southern sub-Saharan Africa
92. **Roseate spoonbill** | *Platalea ajaja* | Bird | Found in fresh-water and saltwater wetland in the USA and South America
93. **Greater rhea** | *Rhea americana* | Bird | Found in grassland, open woodland and saline marshes in south-eastern South America

94. **Southern cassowary** | *Casuarius casuarius* | Bird | Found in lowland rainforest and sometimes in forest, savanna, palm scrub and swamps from New Guinea to Cape York, Australia

95. **Emu** | *Dromaius novaehollandiae* | Bird | Found in dry forest and savanna woodland in mainland Australia

Homebodies

96. **World's smallest land snail** | *Angustopila dominikae* | Mollusc | Found in limestone peaks in Guangxi, southern China

97. **Hairy snail** | *Trochulus hispidus* | Mollusc | Found in a variety of wet, shaded habitats in Europe

98. **Garden snail** | *Helix aspersa* | Mollusc | Found in forest, farmland and gardens on all continents except Antarctica

99. **Brown-lipped snail** | *Cepaea nemoralis* | Mollusc | Found in many habitats – hedgerows, woodland and grassland – in Europe and North America

100. **Cuban painted snail** | *Polymita picta iolimbata* | Mollusc | Found on trees in eastern Cuba | C

101. **Ecuadorian hermit crab** | *Coenobita compressus* | Crustacean | Found in moist thick vegetation and sandy beaches from western USA to Chile

102. **Ruggie** | *Coenobita rugosus* | Crustacean | Found on beaches and coastal vegetation from western Africa to Australia, the Pacific and eastern North America

103. **Candy-cane snail** | *Liguus virgineus* | Mollusc | Found in trees on the island of Hispaniola in the Caribbean

104. **Australian land hermit crab** | *Coenobita variabilis* | Crustacean | Found in mangroves and beaches along the northern coast of Australia

105. **Cuvier tropid snail** | *Tropidophora cuvieriana* | Mollusc | Found in dry forest in Madagascar

106. **Strawberry hermit crab** | *Coenobita perlatus* | Crustacean | Found in coastal shorelines from the Indo-Pacific islands to Samoa

107. **Giant flat snail** | *Caracolus excellens* | Mollusc | Found in vegetation in the Dominican Republic

108. **Speckled dwarf tortoise** | *Chersobius signatus* | Reptile | Found in shrubland and rocky areas in western South Africa | E

109. **Black-knobbed map turtle** | *Graptemys nigrinoda* | Reptile | Found in subtropical and tropical forest and wetlands in southern North America

110. **Ornate box turtle** | *Terrapene ornate* | Reptile | Found in grassland and sand dunes in North America

111. **Yellow-bellied slider** | *Trachemys scripta scripta* | Reptile | Found in freshwater and brackish environments in southern and central USA and northern Mexico

112. **Giant African snail** | *Achatina fulica* | Mollusc | Found in tropical habitats in East Africa by waterways, in coastal and agricultural areas, wetlands and forest

113. **Diamondback terrapin** | *Malaclemys terrapin* | Reptile | Found in saltwater habitats near fresh drinking water on the eastern coast of the USA | V

114. **Painted wood turtle** | *Rhinoclemmys pulcherrima* | Reptile | Found in moist woodland, scrubland, and forest near streams from Mexico to Costa Rica

115. **Californian desert tortoise** | *Gopherus agassizii* | Reptile | Found in thorn scrub and desert scrub in south-western USA and north-western Mexico | V

116. **Star tortoise** | *Geochelone elegans* | Reptile | Found in forest, arid grassland and semidesert in India, Pakistan and Sri Lanka | V

117. **North American wood turtle** | *Glyptemys insculpta* | Reptile | Found in streams, creeks and rivers in eastern Canada and north-eastern USA | E

118. **Leopard tortoise** | *Psammobates pardalis* | Reptile | Found in shrub habitat, dry arid plains and temperate grassland in Africa

119. **Alligator snapping turtle** | *Macrochelys temminckii* | Reptile | Found in large rivers, canals, lakes and swamps in southern USA | V

120. **Aldabra giant tortoise** | *Aldabrachelys gigantea* | Reptile | Found in grassland, scrub forest, mangrove swamps, dunes and beaches on the Aldabra Atoll, Seychelles | V

121. **Galapagos tortoise** | *Chelonoidis nigra* | Reptile | Found in arid grassy lowland areas and swimming in volcanic highlands in the Galapagos Islands | C / E

Legless Legends

122. **California legless lizard** | *Anniella pulchra* | Reptile | Found in coastal dunes in California and Mexico

123. **Striped legless lizard** | *Delma impar* | Reptile | Found in native grassland in south-eastern Australia

124. **Darevsky's viper** | *Vipera darevskii* | Reptile | Found in rocky mountainous parts of Armenia, Turkey and Georgia | C

125. **Slender glass lizard** | *Ophisaurus attenuatus* | Reptile | Found in grassland, woods, sand prairies and pine barrens in North America

126. **Red corn snake** | *Pantherophis guttatus* | Reptile | Found in woods, rocky hillsides, meadows and derelict buildings in eastern USA

127. **Burton's legless lizard** | *Lialis burtonis* | Reptile | Found in many habitats from desert to rainforest in Papua New Guinea and mainland Australia

128. **African bush viper** | *Atheris squamigera* | Reptile | Found in tropical forest and dense vegetation in western and central Africa

129. **Common death adder** | *Acanthophis antarcticus* | Reptile | Found in many habitats from rainforest to woodland, shrubland, grassland and heathland in Australia

130. **Antiguan racer** | *Alsophis antiguae* | Reptile | Found in woodland with dense vegetation, sandy beaches and rocky outcrops on Caribbean islands | C

131. **California kingsnake** | *Lampropeltis californiae* | Reptile | Found in many habitats from desert to grassland, farmland, marshland, woods and suburbia in western USA and Mexico

132. **Wagner's viper** | *Montivipera wagneri* | Reptile | Found in rocky and grassy habitat in the mountains of Turkey and Iran | C

133. **Tiger snake** | *Notechis scutatus* | Reptile | Found in many habitats from forest to woodland, grassland, heath, wetlands and beside creeks in Australia

134. **Scheltopusik** | *Pseudopus apodus* | Reptile | Found in many habitats both dry and wet from eastern Europe to Asia

135. **Paradise flying snake** | *Chrysopelea paradisi* | Reptile | Found in rainforest, deciduous forest, mangroves, parks and gardens in South-East Asia

136. **Green tree python** | *Morelia viridis* | Reptile | Found in lowland rainforest and regrowth forest in New Guinea and Cape York, Australia

137. **Red-bellied black snake** | *Pseudechis porphyriacus* | Reptile | Found near streams, swamps and lagoons in forest, woodland, grassland and farms in eastern Australia

138. **Aruba Island rattlesnake** | *Crotalus unicolor* | Reptile | Found in arid sandy or rocky hillsides on islands of the West Indies | C

139. **Green anaconda** | *Eunectes murinus* | Reptile | Found in freshwater habitats, tropical savanna, grassland and rainforest in the tropical lowlands of South America

140. **Eastern brown snake** | *Pseudonaja textilis* | Reptile | Found everywhere but rainforest and alpine areas, preferring open woodland,

scrubland, grassland, wetlands and farms in eastern Australia

141. **Yellow anaconda** | *Eunectes notaeus* | Reptile | Found in swamps, marshland and forest near rivers and streams in southern South America

Magic Mimics

142. **Baron caterpillar** | *Euthalia aconthea* | Insect | Found in tropical rainforest, mango and cashew orchards and gardens from India to South-East Asia

143. **Leaf-mimicking katydid** | *Eulophophyllum kirki* | Insect | Found in lowland forest in the Danum Valley, Sabah, Malaysia

144. **Smallest chameleon** | *Brookesia micra* | Reptile | Found in leaf litter in dry forest on eroded limestone outcrops on Nosy Hara island off Madagascar

145. **Giant dead-leaf mantis** | *Deroplatys desiccata* | Insect | Found in forest and scrubland in Borneo, Indonesia, Malaysia and the Philippines

146. **Orchid mantis** | *Hymenopus coronatus* | Insect | Found in rainforest in South-East Asia and Indonesia

147. **Orange oakleaf butterfly** | *Kallima inachus* | Insect | Found in tropical deciduous and subtropical evergreen forest in mountainous country from India to Japan and South-East Asia

148. **Günther's leaf-tailed gecko** | *Uroplatus guentheri* | Reptile | Found in deciduous forest in western Madagascar | E

149. **Giant owl butterfly** | *Caligo memnon* | Insect | Found in near banana crops and other agriculture areas in Central and South America

150. **Giant Malaysian leaf insect** | *Phyllium giganteum* | Insect | Found in tropical rainforest canopy in Malaysia

151. **Jewelled chameleon** | *Furcifer campani* | Reptile | Found in shrubland and grassland in Madagascar | V

152. **Giant prickly stick insect** | *Extatosoma tiaratum* | Insect | Found in tropical eucalyptus forest in Australia and New Guinea

153. **Satanic leaf-tailed gecko** | *Uroplatus phantasticus* | Reptile | Found in tropical forest canopy in Madagascar

154. **Lined leaf-tailed gecko** | *Uroplatus lineatus* | Reptile | Found in humid tropical and bamboo forest of eastern Madagascar

155. **Henkel's leaf-tailed gecko** | *Uroplatus henkeli* | Reptile | Found in lowland rainforest in Madagascar | V

156. **Tokay gecko** | *Gekko gecko* | Reptile | Found in trees and on cliffs in tropical rainforest, and as pets, from north-eastern India to Thailand

157. **California ground squirrel** | *Spermophilus beecheyi* | Mammal | Found in grassland and woodland in most of California, western Oregon and parts of western Nevada, USA

158. **Panther chameleon** | *Furcifer pardalis* | Reptile | Found in dry lowland deciduous forest in Madagascar

159. **Veiled chameleon** | *Chamaeleo calyptratus* | Reptile | Found in trees on high plateaus between Yemen and Saudi Arabia

160. **Arctic fox** | *Vulpes lagopus* | Mammal | Found in tundra in arctic regions of Eurasia, North America, Greenland and Iceland

161. **Arctic hare** | *Lepus arcticus* | Mammal | Found in mountainous tundra, rocky plateaus and coasts within the Arctic Circle

162. **Polar bear** | *Ursus maritimus* | Mammal | Found on pack ice in the Arctic Ocean | V

163. **Okapi** | *Okapia johnstoni* | Mammal | Found in rainforest in the Democratic Republic of the Congo | E

Spikey Spunks

164. **Io moth caterpillar** | *Automeris io* | Insect | Found in deciduous woodland, forest, meadows, orchards, parks and backyards in eastern North America

165. **Spined micrathena spider** | *Micrathena gracilis* | Arachnid | Found in dense deciduous forest in eastern USA

166. **Four-spined jewel spider** | *Gasteracantha quadrispinosa* | Arachnid | Found in tropical rainforest in Queensland, Australia

167. **Armadillo lizard** | *Ouroborus cataphractus* | Reptile | Found in rocky outcrops in semidesert regions on the west coast of South Africa

168. **Lowland streaked tenrec** | *Hemicentetes semispinosus* | Mammal | Found in tropical rainforest in Madagascar

169. **Thorny devil** | *Moloch horridus* | Reptile | Found in arid and semi-arid regions with mallee scrub, spinifex or sandy ridges in the Great Sandy Desert in Australia

170. **Echidna** | *Tachyglossus aculeatus* | Monotreme mammal | Found in arid to temperate, coastal to alpine regions throughout Australia and south-eastern New Guinea

171. **Guinea turaco** | *Tauraco persa* | Bird | Found in lowland forest and savanna mainly in western Africa

172. **Sulphur-crested cockatoo** | *Cacatua galerita* | Bird | Found in many habitats from arid areas to urban parks and gardens in eastern and northern Australia, Papua New Guinea and now New Zealand

173. **Golden spiny mouse** | *Acomys russatus* | Mammal | Found in desert and savanna in the Middle East and Africa

174. **Spiny turtle** | *Heosemys spinosa* | Reptile | Found in rainforest near water in South-East Asia | E

175. **Greater sage-grouse** | *Centrocercus urophasianus* | Bird | Found in sagebrush habitat, wetlands and wet meadows in North America

176. **Macaroni penguin** | *Eudyptes chrysolophus* | Bird | Found on the rocky coasts of subantarctic islands to the Antarctic Peninsula | V

177. **Bare-faced curassow** | *Crax fasciolata* | Bird | Found in humid gallery forest in central South America | V

178. **Black-crowned crane** | *Balearica pavonina* | Bird | Found in wetlands, marshes, ponds, lakes and rivers in central Africa | V

Swingers and Clingers

179. **Ring-tailed lemur** | *Lemur catta* | Mammal | Found in continuous canopy forest, brush and scrub forest and mixed forest in southern and south-western Madagascar | E

180. **Black-and-white ruffed lemur** | *Varecia variegata* | Mammal | Found in tropical rainforest in eastern Madagascar | C

181. **Bolivian squirrel monkey** | *Saimiri boliviensis* | Mammal | Found in tropical rainforest and forest edges in Brazil, Bolivia and Peru

182. **De Brazza's monkey** | *Cercopithecus neglectus* | Mammal | Found in forest, swamps, bamboo and dry mountain forest in central-western Africa

183. **White-handed gibbon** | *Hylobates lar* | Mammal | Found in tropical rainforest in South-East Asia | E

184. **Chimpanzee** | *Pan troglodytes* | Mammal | Found in tropical forest in central Africa | E

185. **Southern two-toed sloth** | *Choloepus didactylus* | Mammal | Found in tropical rainforest in Central America and northern South America

186. **Lumholtz's tree kangaroo** | *Dendrolagus lumholtzi* | Marsupial mammal | Found in upland tropical rainforest in north-eastern Australia

187. **Goodfellow's tree kangaroo** | *Dendrolagus goodfellowi* | Marsupial mammal | Found in tropical rainforest in Papua New Guinea | E

188. **Red ruffed lemur** | *Varecia rubra* | Mammal | Found in tropical deciduous forest in north-eastern Madagascar | C

189. **Siamang gibbon** | *Symphalangus syndactylus* | Mammal | Found in mountain,

hill and lowland rainforest in Sumatra, Indonesia; Thailand and Malaysia | E

190. **Proboscis monkey** | *Nasalis larvatus* | Mammal | Found in lowland rainforest, mangroves and swamps in Borneo | E

191. **Koala** | *Phascolarctos cinereus* | Marsupial mammal | Found in eucalyptus forest in Australia | V

192. **Coquerel's mouse lemur** | *Propithecus coquereli* | Mammal | Found in dry deciduous and evergreen forest in northern Madagascar | C

193. **Brown-throated three-toed sloth** | *Bradypus variegatus* | Mammal | Found in tropical rainforest, forest, subtropical lowlands and swamps in South America and southern Central America

194. **Borneo orangutan** | *Pongo pygmaeus* | Mammal | Found in tropical rainforest and swamps in Borneo | C

Spotted Bottoms

195. **Rusty-spotted cat** | *Prionailurus rubiginosus* | Mammal | Found in dry forest habitat in Sri Lanka and India

196. **Western spotted skunk** | *Spilogale gracilis* | Mammal | Found in rocky habitats and brush beside canyon streams in western North America

197. **Spotted lanternfly** | *Lycorma delicatula* | Insect | Found on vines and trees, especially the tree of heaven, in China, India and Vietnam

198. **Red avadavat** | *Amandava amandava* | Bird | Found in grassy areas and near water in southern Asia and South-East Asia

199. **Eastern spotted salamander** | *Ambystoma maculatum* | Amphibian | Found in deciduous forest near water, damp mixed or coniferous forest in eastern North America

200. **Spotted wood kingfisher** | *Actenoides lindsayi* | Bird | Found in tropical or subtropical rainforest in the Philippines

201. **Tiger quoll** | *Dasyurus maculatus* | Marsupial mammal | Found in rainforest, forest, woodland and paddocks in Australia

202. **Eastern quoll** | *Dasyurus viverrinus* | Marsupial mammal | Found in rainforest, woodland and forest with dense canopies in Tasmania, Australia | E

203. **Spotted linsang** | *Prionodon pardicolor* | Mammal | Found in dense tropical forest and dryer habitats in South-East Asia

204. **African civet** | *Civettictis civetta* | Mammal | Found in forest and savanna in southern and central Africa

205. **Temminck's tragopan** | *Tragopan temminckii* | Bird | Found in temperate forest and shrubland in China, India, Myanmar and Vietnam

206. **Common genet** | *Genetta genetta* | Mammal | Found in forest in northern Africa and Europe

207. **Dalmatian dog** | *Canis lupus familiaris* | Mammal | Found with people throughout the world

208. **Brazilian tapir baby** | *Tapirus terrestris* | Mammal | Found in tropical forest in mountains, lowlands and swamps in South America, mainly Brazil | V

209. **Spotted hyena** | *Crocuta crocuta* | Mammal | Found in open, dry habitat such as semidesert, savanna and forested mountains in sub-Saharan Africa

210. **Helmeted guinea fowl** | *Numida meleagris* | Bird | Found in savanna or farmland in sub-Saharan Africa, and widely domesticated

211. **Visayan spotted deer** | *Rusa alfredi* | Mammal | Found in tropical forest in central Philippines | E

212. **Harbour seal** | *Phoca vitulina* | Mammal | Found in shallow waters on most coasts of the northern hemisphere and even freshwater rivers

213. **Cheetah** | *Acinonyx jubatus* | Mammal | Found in grassland and desert in parts of Africa and southern Asia | V

214. **Leopard seal** | *Hydrurga leptonyx* | Mammal | Found in Antarctic pack ice and subantarctic islands

215. **Holstein–Friesian cow** | *Bos taurus taurus* | Mammal | Found on pasture in Holland and Friesland, Netherlands, originally; now widespread and domesticated

216. **Sika deer** | *Cervus nippon* | Mammal | Found in forest, marshes and grassland in eastern Siberia, China, Japan, Korea and Vietnam originally; now widespread and domesticated

217. **American appaloosa horse** | *Equus ferus caballus* | Mammal | Found in grassland in North America originally; now widespread and domesticated

Horny Herbivores

218. **Kirk's dik-dik** | *Madoqua kirkii* | Mammal | Found in arid country with thick shrubs from south-eastern Somalia to central Tanzania and south-western Angola to Namibia

219. **Chinkara** | *Gazella bennettii* | Mammal | Found in dry and arid habitats from forest to desert in north-western India, Pakistan, Afghanistan and Iran

220. **Scottish highland cow** | *Bos taurus* | Mammal | Found in the highlands and west coast islands of Scotland originally; now widespread and domesticated

221. **Nubian ibex** | *Capra nubiana* | Mammal | Found in mountains with little vegetation in coastal north-eastern Africa, the Sinai Peninsula and south-eastern and western Arabian Peninsula | V

222. **Impala** | *Aepyceros melampus* | Mammal | Found in woodland and grassland mainly in south-eastern Africa

223. **Pronghorn** | *Antilocapra americana* | Mammal | Found in prairies, grassland and desert in North America

224. **Saiga** | *Saiga tatarica* | Mammal | Found in dry steppes, semidesert and grassland in Mongolia, Kazakhstan and Kalmykia, Russia | C

225. **Greater kudu** | *Tragelaphus strepsiceros* | Mammal | Found in deciduous woodland and along rivers in eastern and southern Africa

226. **Gemsbok** | *Oryx gazella* | Mammal | Found in grassland, arid dunes and rocky mountains in south-eastern Africa originally; now in Mexico and south-western USA

227. **Bongo** | *Tragelaphus eurycerus* | Mammal | Found in lowland forest and some mountain forest mostly in western and central Africa

228. **Giant eland** | *Taurotragus derbianus* | Mammal | Found in savanna, grassland and sparse forest from Senegal to southern Sudan | V

229. **Ankole-Watusi cattle** | *Bos taurus* | Mammal | Found in grassland and forest meadows in Uganda, Tanzania, Rwanda and Burundi; domesticated

230. **White rhinoceros** | *Ceratotherium simum* | Mammal | Found in dense forest, savanna and grassy woodland in southern and central Africa

Woolly Wanderers

231. **Suffolk sheep** | *Ovis aries* | Mammal | Found in pasture in England originally; now widespread and domesticated

232. **French angora rabbit** | *Oryctolagus cuniculus* | Mammal | Found in fields and forest in Turkey originally; now widespread and domesticated

233. **Guanaco** | *Lama guanicoe* | Mammal | Found in open dry habitat but tolerates extremes, from desert to wet forest, south from northern Peru in South America

234. **Vicuña** | *Vicugna vicugna* | Mammal | Found in semi-arid grassland in mountains in Bolivia, Peru, Chile, Argentina and Ecuador

235. **Cashmere goat** | *Capra hircus* | Mammal | Found in pasture in India originally; now widespread and domesticated

236. **Angora goat** | *Capra hircus* | Mammal | Found in pasture in Turkey originally; now widespread and domesticated

237. **Jacob sheep** | *Ovis aries* | Mammal | Found in pasture in Britain originally, but now more widespread in Europe and North America; domesticated

238. **Alpaca** | *Lama pacos* | Mammal | Found in high plateaus and pasture in the central and southern Andes mountains originally; now widespread and domesticated

239. **Llama** | *Lama glama* | Mammal | Found in pasture in the Andes mountains originally; now widespread and domesticated

240. **Wensleydale sheep** | *Ovis aries* | Mammal | Found in pasture in Britain originally; domesticated

241. **Icelandic sheep** | *Ovis aries* | Mammal | Found in pasture in northern Europe originally, but now more widespread; domesticated

242. **Bighorn sheep** | *Ovis canadensis* | Mammal | Found in alpine meadows and foothills near rocky cliffs in North America

243. **Musk ox** | *Ovibos moschatus* | Mammal | Found in arctic tundra in Canada, Greenland and Alaska, USA, originally; now in Russia, Norway, Sweden and Siberia

244. **Wild yak** | *Bos mutus* | Mammal | Found in alpine meadows and desert steppes on the high plateau that stretches from India to China | V

245. **Bactrian camel** | *Camelus bactrianus* | Mammal | Found in rocky mountains, desert, sand dunes and stony plains in central Asia and north-western China originally; now domesticated

Growlers and Howlers

246. **Growling grass frog** | *Litoria raniformis* | Amphibian | Found in dams, ponds, swamps and marshes in south-eastern Australia | E

247. **Meerkat** | *Suricata suricatta* | Mammal | Found in open and arid country in Angola, Botswana, Namibia, Mozambique and South Africa

248. **Groundhog** | *Marmota monax* | Mammal | Found in forest, woodlots, fields and hedgerows in North America

249. **Honey badger** | *Mellivora capensis* | Mammal | Found in tropical and subtropical forest, woodland, grassland, rocky hills, arid steppes and desert in Africa, Europe and Asia

250. **Mantled howler monkey** | *Alouatta palliata* | Mammal | Found in rainforest in Mexico, and Central and South America | V

251. **Dhole** | *Cuon alpinus* | Mammal | Found in forest, jungle clearings and shrubland, but not deserts or open plains, in central, southern and South-East Asia | E

252. **Dingo** | *Canis lupus dingo* | Mammal | Found in forest, desert, shrubland and grassland in Australia, Malaysia, Thailand, Philippines and New Guinea | V

253. **African wild dog** | *Lycaon pictus* | Mammal | Found in woodland, grassland and savanna scattered through Africa | E

254. **Arctic wolf** | *Canis lupus arctos* | Mammal | Found in arctic tundra in Canada and Greenland

255. **Grey wolf** | *Canis lupus* | Mammal | Found in habitats from arctic tundra to arid regions, forest and grassland in North America, Europe, the Middle East and Asia

256. **Tibetan mastiff** | *Canis lupus familiaris* | Mammal | Originally found in the Himalayas in East Asia through to Mongolia, but now more widespread; domesticated

257. **Wolverine** | *Gulo gulo* | Mammal | Found in alpine forest, tundra or grassland in Scandinavia, Russia and North America

258. **American black bear** | *Ursus americanus* | Mammal | Found in inaccessible mountainous places with thick vegetation in North and Central America

259. **Asiatic black bear** | *Ursus thibetanus* | Mammal | Found in moist forest, thick vegetation and steep mountains in Asia from Pakistan to Japan | V

260. **Brown bear** | *Ursus arctos* | Mammal | Found in habitats from desert edges to mountain forest, tundra and meadows from Western Europe to the Himalayas and northern Japan

Big, Bold and Beautiful

261. **Goliath beetle** | *Goliathus albosignatus* | Insect | Found in rainforest in south-eastern Africa

262. **Giant grasshopper** | *Valanga irregularis* | Insect | Found in grassland, forest and gardens in Australia

263. **Sea slater** | *Ligia oceanica* | Crustacean | Found among rocks on beaches and in rock walls in the United Kingdom and Ireland

264. **Chinese giant salamander** | *Andrias davidianus* | Amphibian | Found in streams, rivers and large lakes in China | C

265. **Giant anteater** | *Myrmecophaga tridactyla* | Mammal | Found in swamps, forest and grassland in Central and South America | V

266. **Giant otter** | *Pteronura brasiliensis* | Mammal | Found in calm rivers, lakes, dams, canals and creeks in South America | E

267. **Goliath birdeater spider** | *Theraphosa blondi* | Arachnid | Found in rainforest in Guyana, French Guiana and Suriname in northern South America

268. **Komodo dragon** | *Varanus komodoensis* | Reptile | Found in tropical savanna, beaches and ridges on Komodo island and neighbouring islands in Indonesia | V

269. **Capybara** | *Hydrochoerus hydrochaeris* | Mammal | Found in forest, scrub and grassland near water in Central and South America

270. **Giant African millipede** | *Archispirostreptus gigas* | Insect | Found in forest in Africa

271. **African giant swallowtail** | *Papilio antimachus* | Insect | Found in tropical rainforest in western and central Africa

272. **Indian rhinoceros** | *Rhinoceros unicornis* | Mammal | Found in alluvial plains but also swamps and forest from northern Pakistan across India and Nepal to Bangladesh | V

273. **Wandering albatross** | *Diomedea exulans* | Bird | Found in southern oceans and islands in the Antarctic Circle and South Atlantic | V

274. **Goliath birdwing** | *Ornithoptera goliath* | Insect | Found in rainforest in Papua New Guinea

275. **Queen Alexandra birdwing butterfly** | *Ornithoptera alexandrae* | Insect | Found in rainforest in Papua New Guinea | E

276. **African bush elephant** | *Loxodonta africana* | Mammal | Found in many habitats from savanna to rainforest, woodland, desert and beaches in central and southern Africa | E

277. **Giraffe** | *Giraffa camelopardalis* | Mammal | Found in arid savanna, grassland and open woodland scattered through sub-Saharan Africa | V

278. **Giant panda** | *Ailuropoda melanoleuca* | Mammal | Found in montane and mixed forest with bamboo stands in central China | V

Thanks to the many patient and encouraging women who worked with me on this wonderful book. Marta Cortada-McCorkell for your hundreds of hours of research and enthusiasm, I couldn't have done it without you. Paulina de Laveaux for your constant support and belief in me, as always. Jess Levine and Lisa Schuurman for picking up the pieces and joining the dots. Thanks to Chloe Lambert for being my fastidious scale checker and Hope Lumsden-Barry for putting up with the tedious amounts of shuffling and title changes. Eternal thanks to my mum and dad for always encouraging me as a little girl to spend time with animals in nature, and my partner Simon for helping me make my wild dreams into reality.

First published in Australia in 2022
by Thames & Hudson Australia Pty Ltd
11 Central Boulevard, Portside Business Park
Port Melbourne, Victoria 3207
ABN: 72 004 751 964

thamesandhudson.com.au

25 24 23 22 5 4 3 2 1

Thames & Hudson Australia wishes to acknowledge that Aboriginal and Torres Strait Islander people are the first storytellers of this nation and the traditional custodians of the land on which we live and work. We acknowledge their continuing culture and pay respect to Elders past, present and future.

ISBN 978-1-760-76243-8

A catalogue record for this book is available from the National Library of Australia

Design: Hope Lumsden-Barry
Editing: Nan McNab
Photography: Matthew Stanton

Printed and bound in China by RR Donnelley

FSC® is dedicated to the promotion of responsible forest management worldwide. This book is made of material from FSC®-certified forests and other controlled sources.

Rainforests

Coastal shrubs and dunes